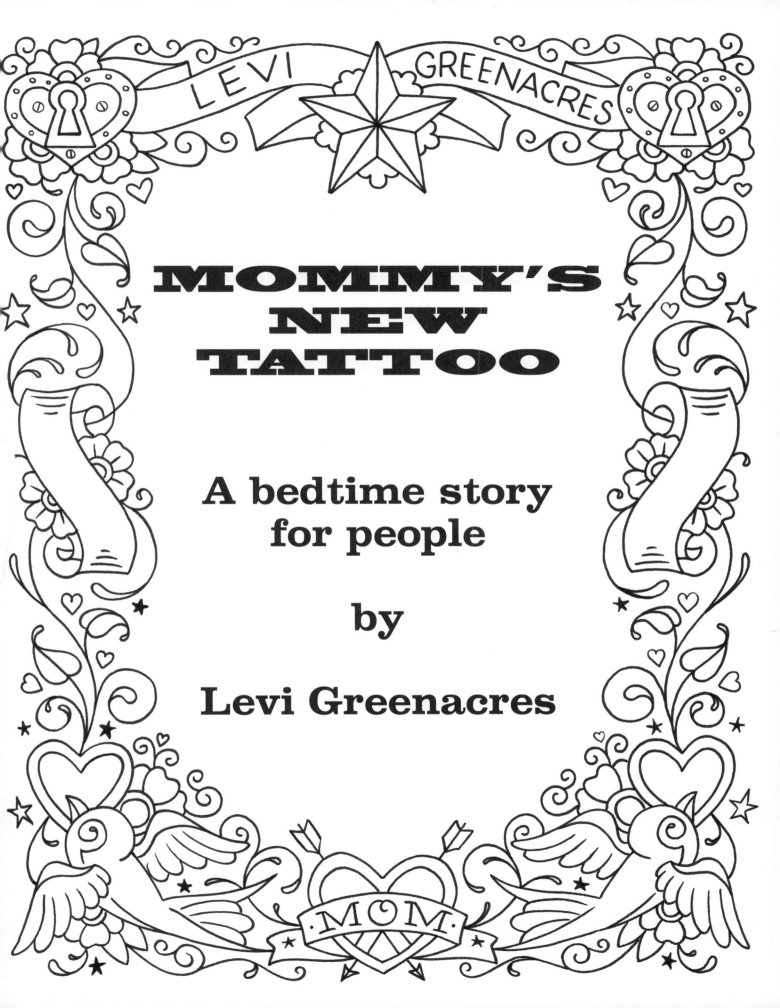

MOMMY'S NEW TATTOO

A bedtime story for people

by

Levi Greenacres

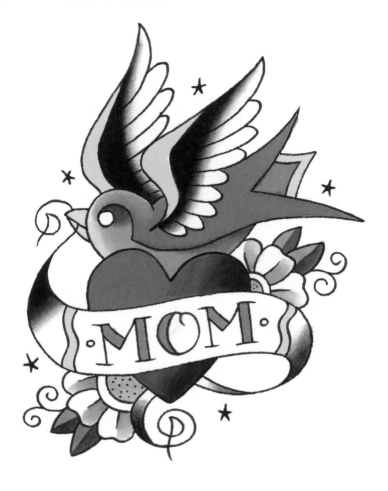

Other Schiffer Books on Related Subjects:

A is for Anchor: A Tattoo Alphabet,
978-0-7643-4386-5, $19.99

Copyright © 2013 by Levi Greenacres

Library of Congress Control Number: 2012952782

Designed by Mark David Bowyer
Type set in Blackoak Std / Clarendon

ISBN: 978-0-7643-4389-6
Printed in China

Schiffer Books are available at special discounts for bulk purchases for sales promotions or premiums. Special editions, including personalized covers, corporate imprints, and excerpts can be created in large quantities for special needs. For more information contact the publisher.

Published by Schiffer Publishing, Ltd.
4880 Lower Valley Road
Atglen, PA 19310
Phone: (610) 593-1777; Fax: (610) 593-2002
E-mail: Info@schifferbooks.com

For the largest selection of fine reference books on this and related subjects, please visit our website at
www.schifferbooks.com.
You may also write for a free catalog.

This book may be purchased from the publisher.
Please try your bookstore first.

We are always looking for people to write books on new and related subjects. If you have an idea for a book, please contact us at
proposals@schifferbooks.com

In Europe, Schiffer books are distributed by
Bushwood Books
6 Marksbury Ave.
Kew Gardens
Surrey TW9 4JF England
Phone: 44 (0) 20 8392 8585; Fax: 44 (0) 20 8392 9876
E-mail: info@bushwoodbooks.co.uk
Website: www.bushwoodbooks.co.uk

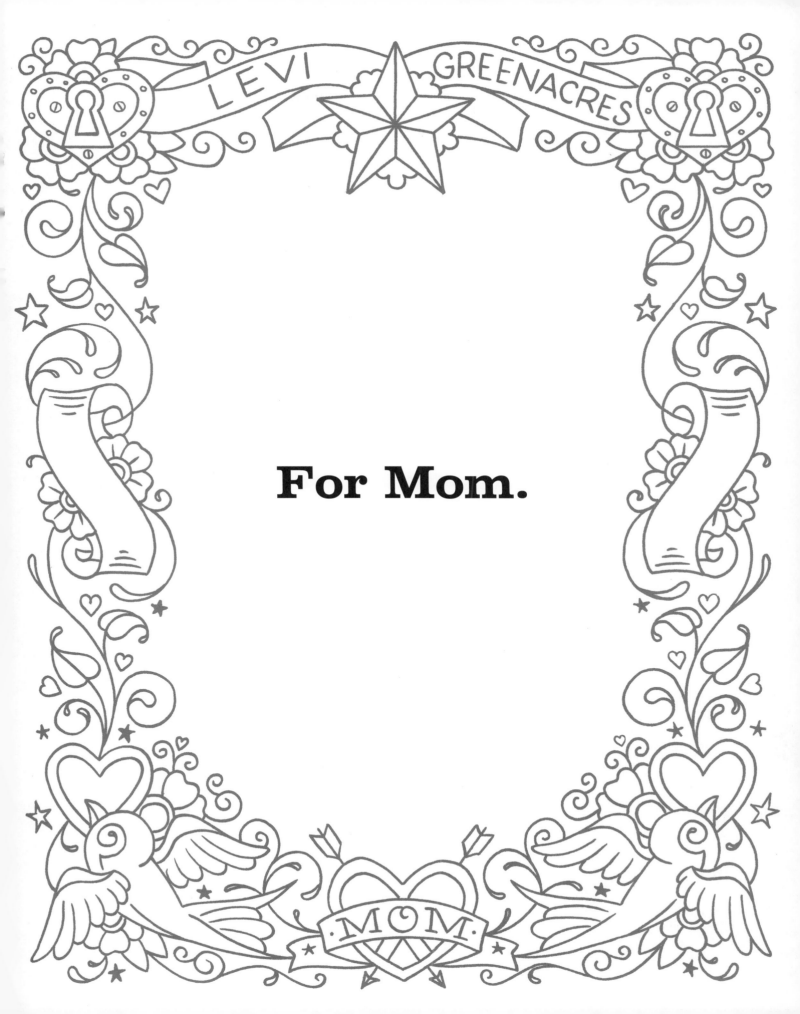

For Mom.

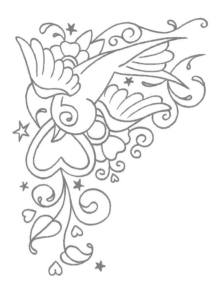

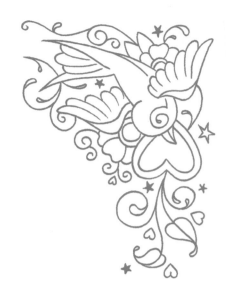

THANKS TO:

Schiffer Publishing; Hubba Hubba at Seattle Tattoo Emporium, Kate Hellenbrand, Mary Jane Haake, Lyle Tuttle, James Bernard Frost, Ryan J. Zeinert, Mark Ledford, and Jake Tong for reviews and encouragement; Julie Gambino for photography and endurance; Andy McGee for being there at the beginning; and friends and family who said, "Go for it."

Thank you to the staff and clients of Skeleton Key Tattoo, for always keeping life interesting.

EXTRA SPECIAL THANKS TO:

Madame Vyvyn Lazonga, for agreeing to be in my book, and giving me a cool tattoo besides.

Katie Williams, for agreeing to be in this book, and for giving great advice about tattooing and a few other things.

Ximena Quiroz, for agreeing to be in my book, running a great tattoo shop I am happy to spend a good deal of time in, and for being a friend.

BG Bryan, for taking me to my first tattoo shop, teaching me how to make country gravy, and how to read—for being the mom in this book and Mom in real life.

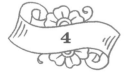

INTRODUCTION

This book started out as a rhyming version of a story I've told many times to my tattoo clients about my first experience in a tattoo shop, as well as a couple of things I've learned about the process of acquiring and displaying visible tattoos. As I put a few versions together on paper, it seemed best that the story be told from the perspective of a person like I was back in 1991 or so: much younger and much farther removed from the idea of a tattoo as an acceptable personal expression—let alone a mainstream cultural phenomenon you could watch on television. No one in my family had or ever would go on to get a tattoo, with the exception of my mother.

My family is originally from various small towns in Oklahoma, where tattooing was illegal until the end of 2006. Much of my young life was lived in ignorance of tattoos. So, going to a tattoo shop in a busy part of a big city was as strange to me then as I imagine now a visit to a carnival on Mars might be. Over the years, more and more people I knew got tattoos. The pictures they chose to wear and the reasons they got them were varied and strange. But nothing was as strange and wonderful as my first visit to Madame Lazonga's Tattoos, which is located now, as it was when I was a kid, in Seattle's Pike Place Market.

Working as a tattooist, collecting lots of pictures and stories of my own, I've enjoyed hearing many of the adventures and thoughts that people have had that led them to get tattoos of their own. One of the reasons given, which is always a pleasure for me to hear, is that they are sharing a tradition and bond with their parents or siblings. While the importance of inclusiveness in certain social groups fades or changes over time, the bond of family belonging is one that we inherit irrevocably for life.

This book is the telling of my own story, and an encouragement to parents to talk to their kids frankly about tattoos and the lifelong commitment they represent. While the ancient practice of tattooing is currently enjoying a social tolerance and celebrity that is unprecedented in human history, as is the distribution of information and myth about the industry and art itself, this may not always be the case. Tattoos can be an ever present reminder of, among other important things, a lady to whom we owe a huge debt of gratitude to for the gift of our existence and nurture, and for the lessons we learned, for better or worse, in our upbringing—our mom.

Getting a tattoo is a highly personal choice. It is not for everyone. To the readers of this book, I advise you when making any decision to ultimately keep your own counsel. Trust your instincts and your heart, and consider the consequences. Whether or not you go on to get a tattoo yourself, I hope you will still enjoy reading *Mommy's New Tattoo*. If you should decide to go ahead and get a tattoo, hopefully you will give the process a little forethought, and choose a piece of art that will reward you with a lifetime of enjoyment.

—**Levi Greenacres**
Portland, Oregon
August 2012

ABOUT THE TATTOO ARTISTS
FEATURED IN THIS BOOK:

MADAME VYVYN LAZONGA has been a tattoo icon for more than 40 years. Beginning in the early 1970s, she was one of maybe two women who were working as tattooists at the time, Kate Hildebrandt being the other, who worked under Sailor Jerry in Honolulu. Vyvyn was one of the first female tattoo artists in the world who went out on her own and didn't work for her husband or partner; she worked for herself and her art. Madame Lazonga has won many awards and has challenged the tattoo and artistic norm, and continues to create amazing custom body art today at her shop in the historic Pike Place Market in Seattle, Washington. Her website is **www.vyvyn.com.**

KATIE WILLIAMS started tattooing in 1990 at the tender age of twenty. Over the past 22 years, she has run a successful parlor, won numerous awards, and produced three children. In her free time, Katie knits, taxis her brood, and plays softball with more vigor than skill. On most days, she can be found at House of Tattoo, in Tacoma, Washington, living the dream. **www.Facebook.com/ HouseofTattooTacoma**

XIMENA QUIROZ thought tattoos were pretty since she was old enough to know that Cracker Jack boxes had them as the toy surprise inside. After growing her personal tattoo and record collections, the winds brought her to The City Of Roses. She apprenticed under Rio DeGenarro in 2006. In 2008, Ximena opened Skeleton Key Tattoo thanks to a kick in the behind from friends and a credit card. Currently she lives in her basement Tiki bar in Portland, Oregon, expanding her record collection and organizing her army of cats. **www.skeletonkeytattooportland.com**

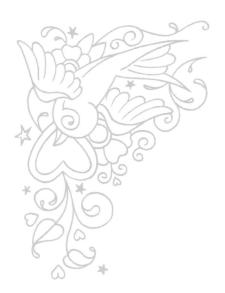

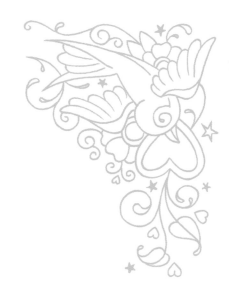

When I was just this tall, I went somewhere special
with my mom to a place in town.
I didn't understand what happened then,
so I made sure to write it down.

Up the stairs from a magician's shop
and a fortune teller's stall,
past the fruit stands in the city market
and its mural-covered walls.

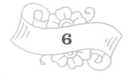

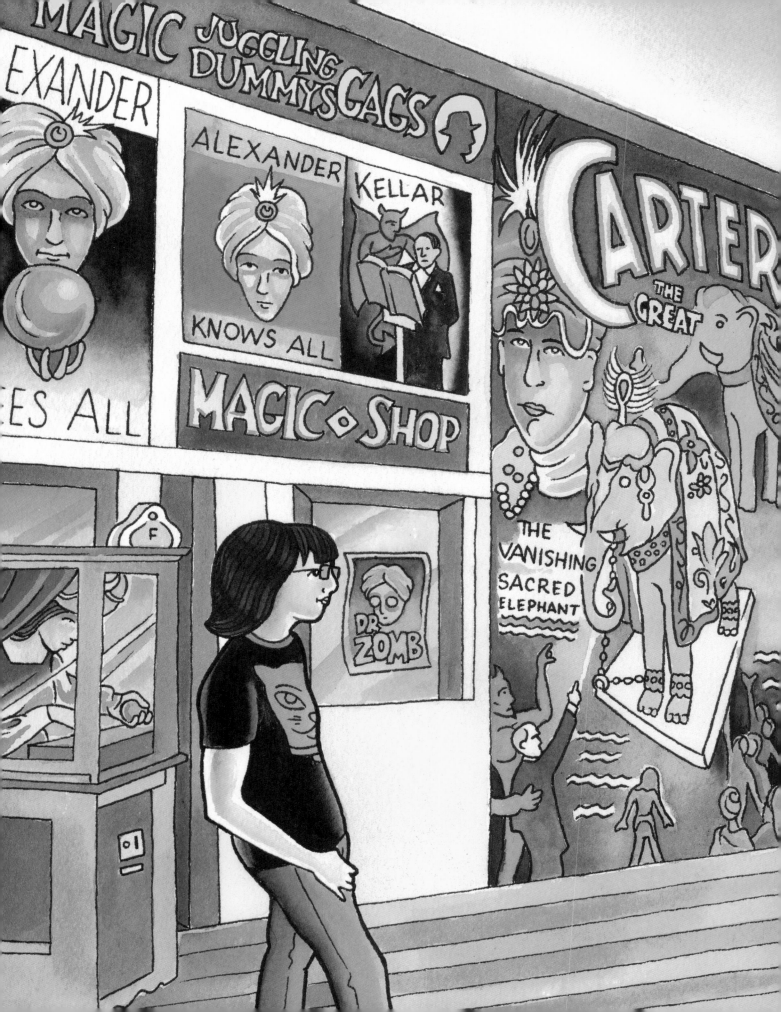

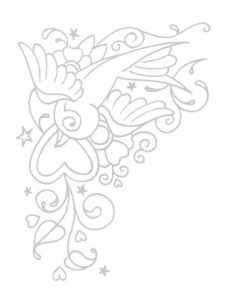

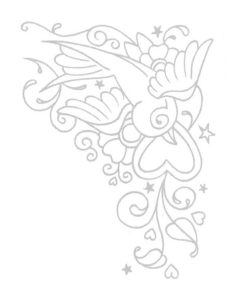

I couldn't wait to see where we were going,
and my curiosity turned to wonder
as we went in through a door under a sign
that read, "Tattoos by Madame Lazonga."

Music came out from somewhere hidden
behind walls filled with pictures old and new.
And I sat on a zebra print sofa and waited
for Mommy to get her new tattoo.

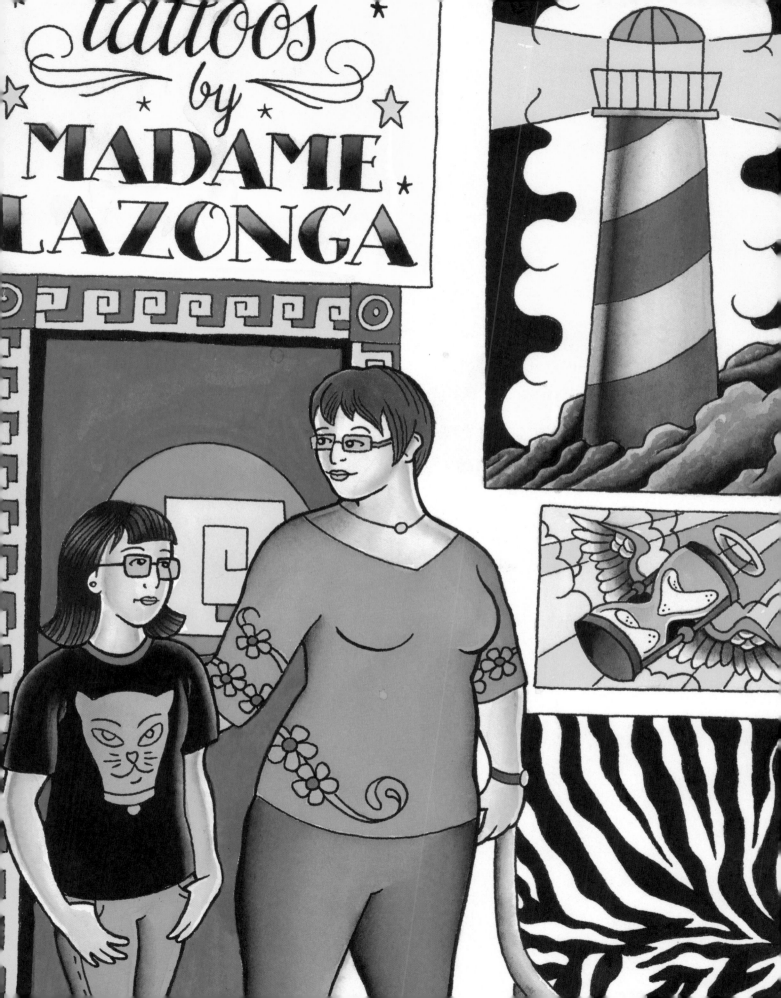

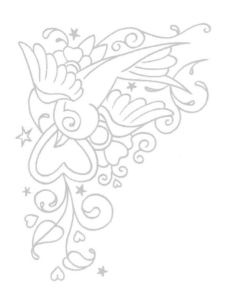

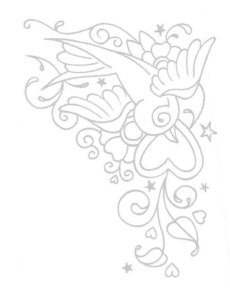

I wanted to touch everything in there,

but I had to be still—a bit hard for me.

Mom told me this was a special place for adults,

so I just used my eyes to see.

There were pictures of panthers and hearts and stars

hung up in a crazy geometry.

Gypsy ladies with their hair piled high

and other things shrouded in mystery.

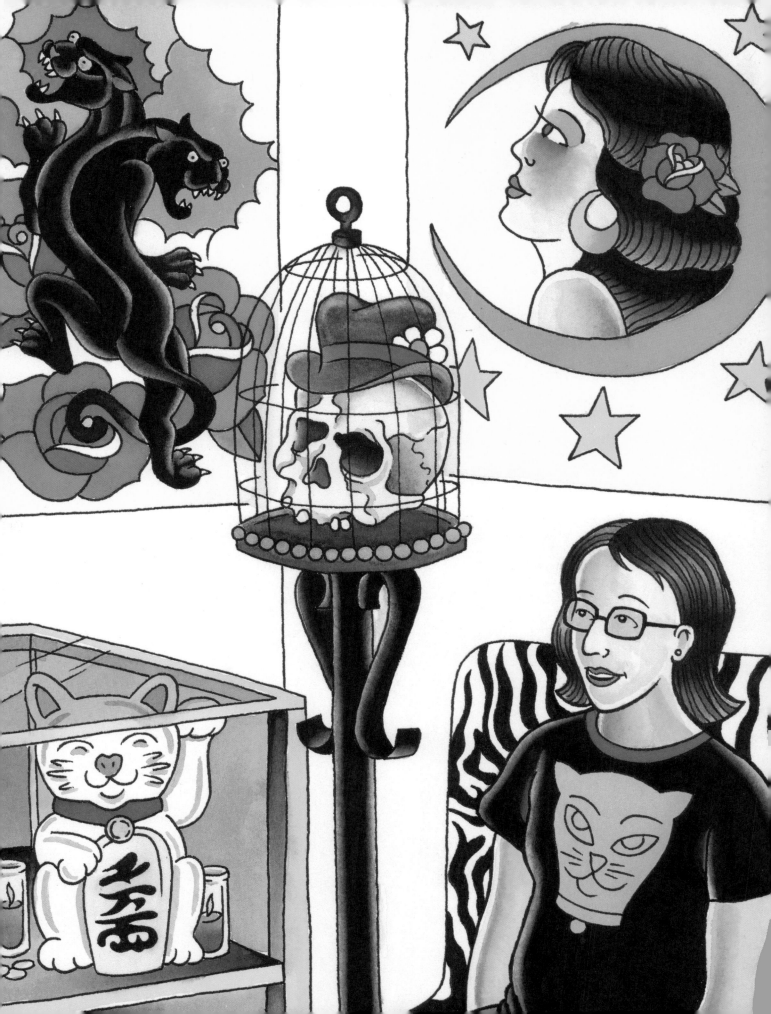

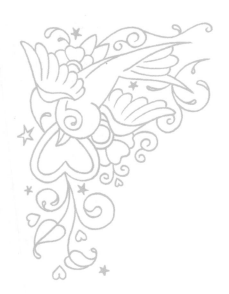
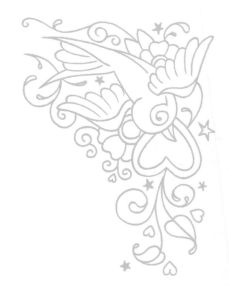

Mom reminded me that I had to be polite,

and we sat and waited a while.

Then out came a lady with storms on her arms,

gloved hands, and a very pretty smile.

They went into a room behind a curtain,

and soon I heard a strange buzzing sound.

Like a giant robot hornet might make

if it were dancing around on the ground.

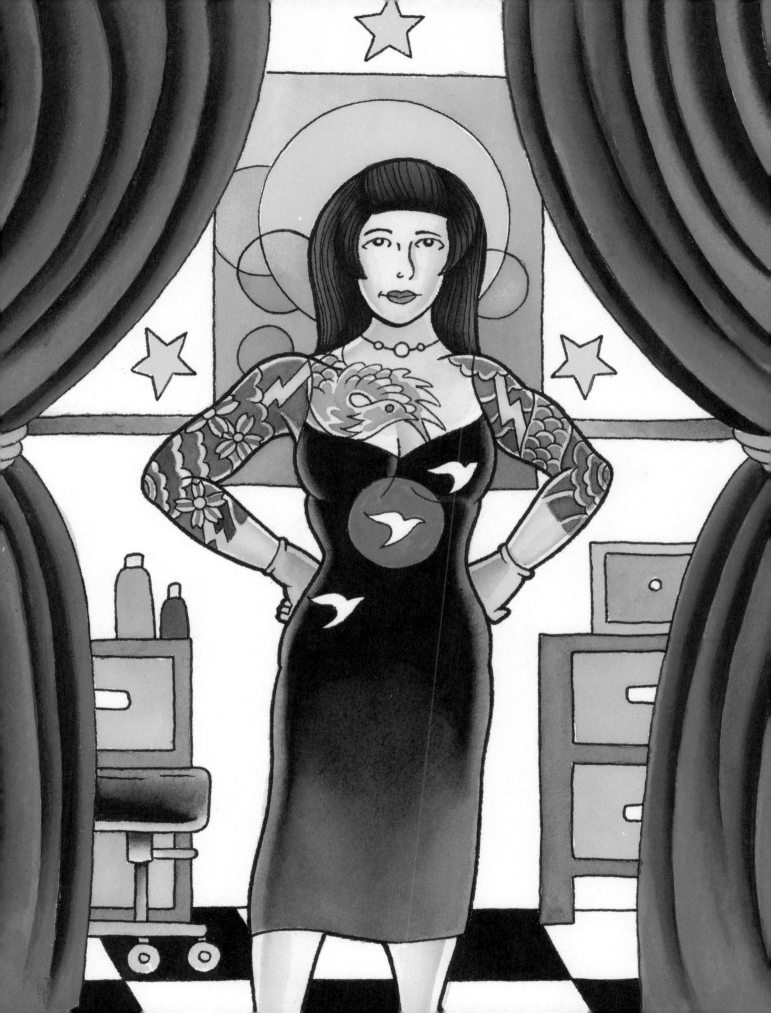

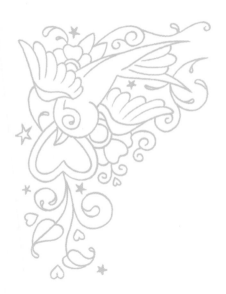

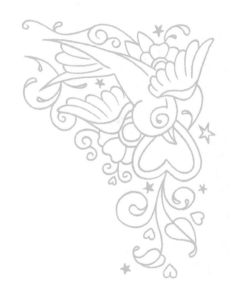

Mom came out a whole hour later,

with a new bandage and a big smile.

"I wanna see it!" I shouted. "Can I see it?" I whispered.

"When we get home," she said, "I'll be wearing my tattoo a while."

Well, I had to wait until the next morning,

after Mommy had her shower,

On her arm was a little bird on a heart that said, "MOM"

and a couple of pretty flowers.

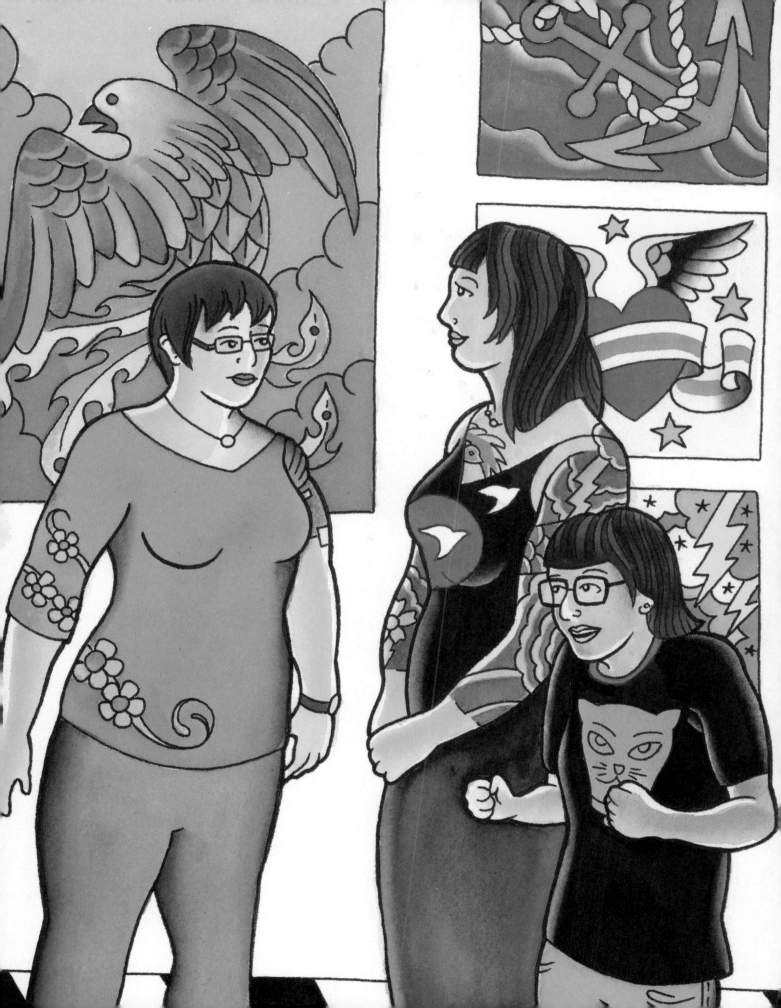

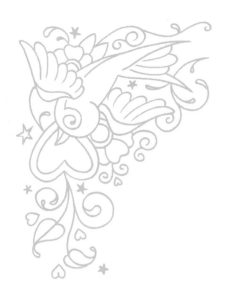

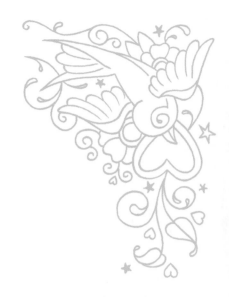

It was so amazing I reached out to touch it,

and Mom said, "It's not healed, so no you don't!"

When I asked her if her bird might fly away,

she said "It's in my skin, so it won't."

"In your skin forever?" I asked.

"It won't ever wash away?"

"That's the best part of a tattoo," she said,

"As long as I'm here, it will stay."

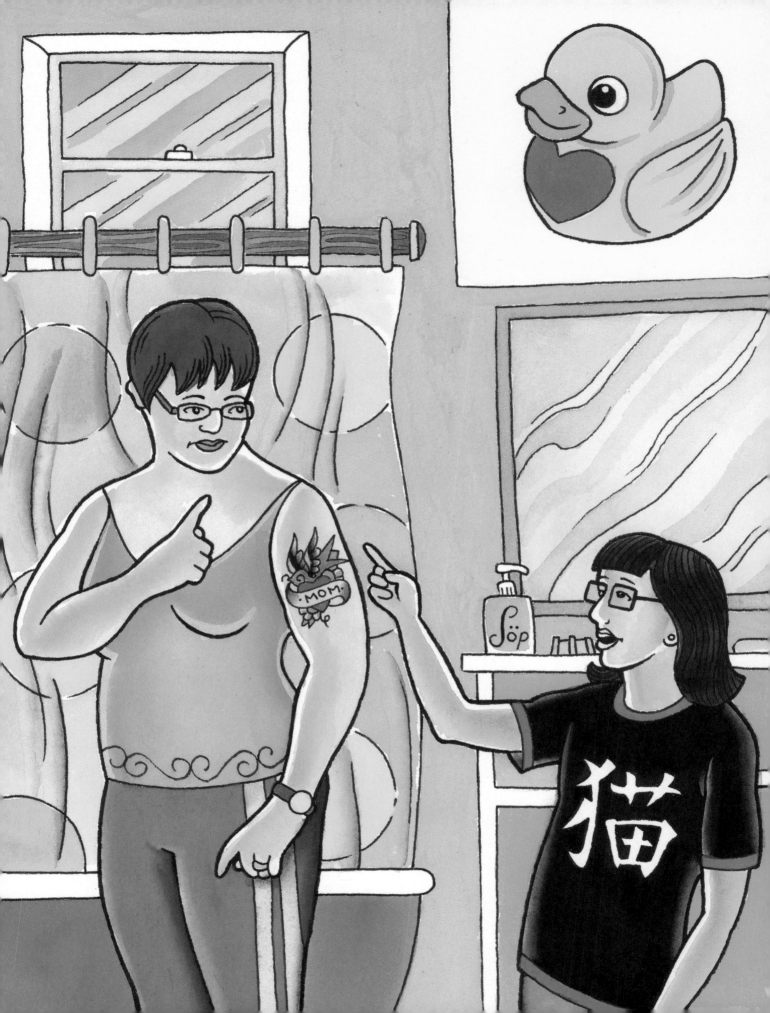

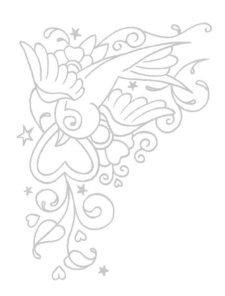

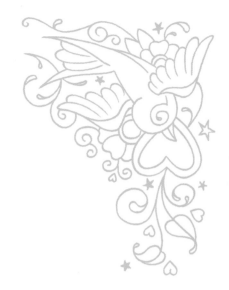

"I got tattooed to remember my mother,

that's why I got something beautiful.

And I also love being your mommy,

and of course I always will.

Some day when you are old enough,

you might decide to get one, too.

Don't be in a hurry because your friends got one,

get a tattoo that's just right for you."

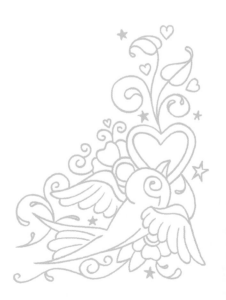

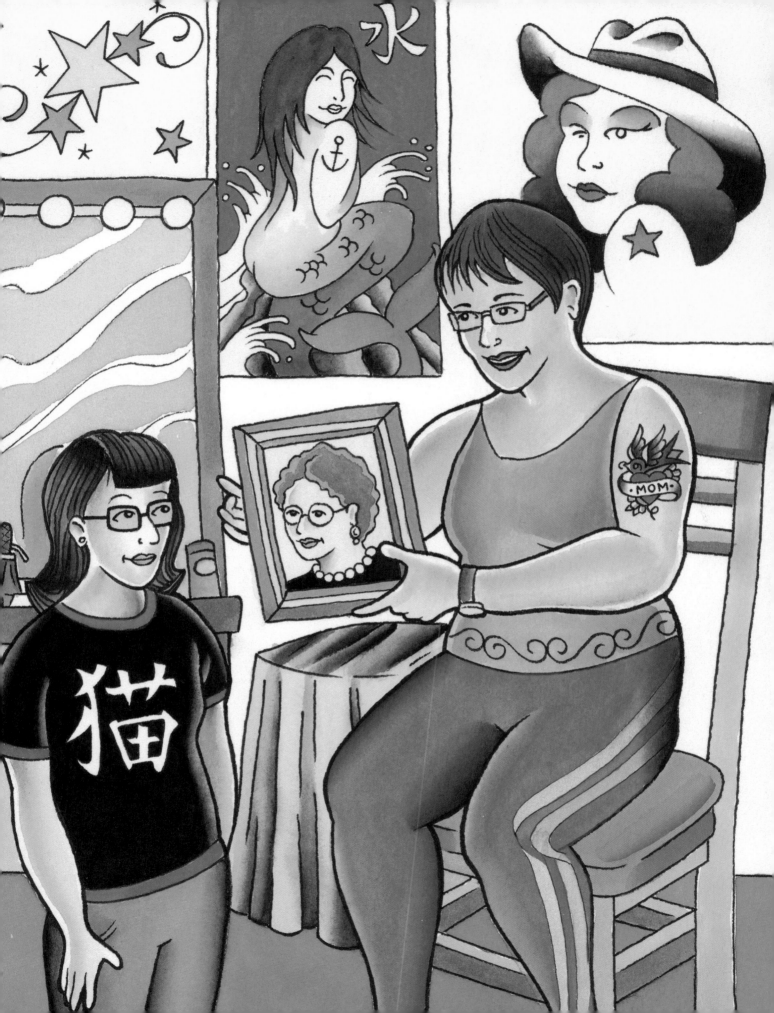

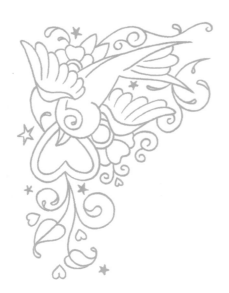
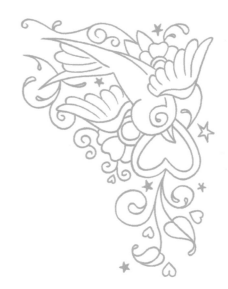

Sometimes people asked Mommy about it,

and said, "Really, now, what will you do?

When you get to be 80,

and every part of you is closer to your shoes?"

"At 80 I'll have more to think about

than all of my skin sagging lower.

I'll do everything I do now," Mom said,

"Except that I'll do it slower."

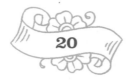

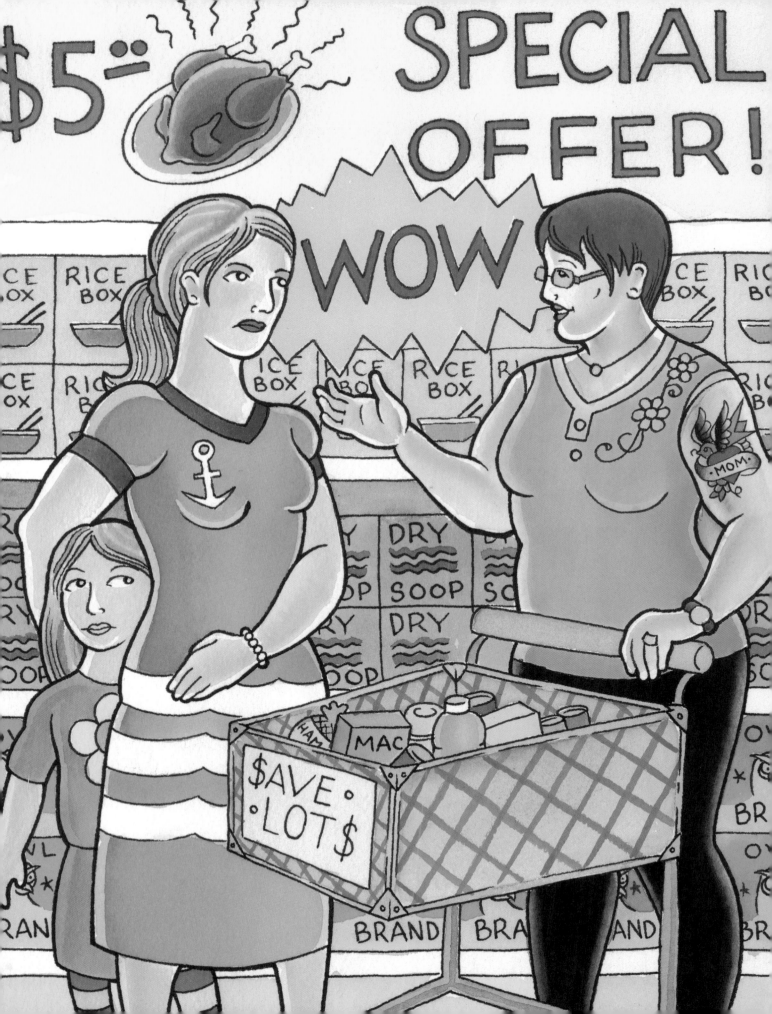

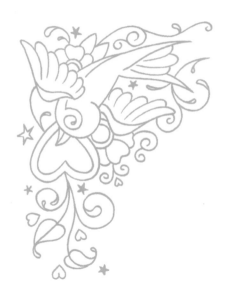

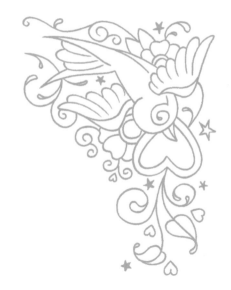

Years later, I saw how her tattoo had changed,

the lines became wider and bigger and blue.

Mom smiled and said, "My wings have spread,

and my heart has grown, just like my love for you."

When I was old enough, I thought and waited

'til I I knew what I wanted to do.

I waited a couple of months to make sure,

and then I went and got tattooed.

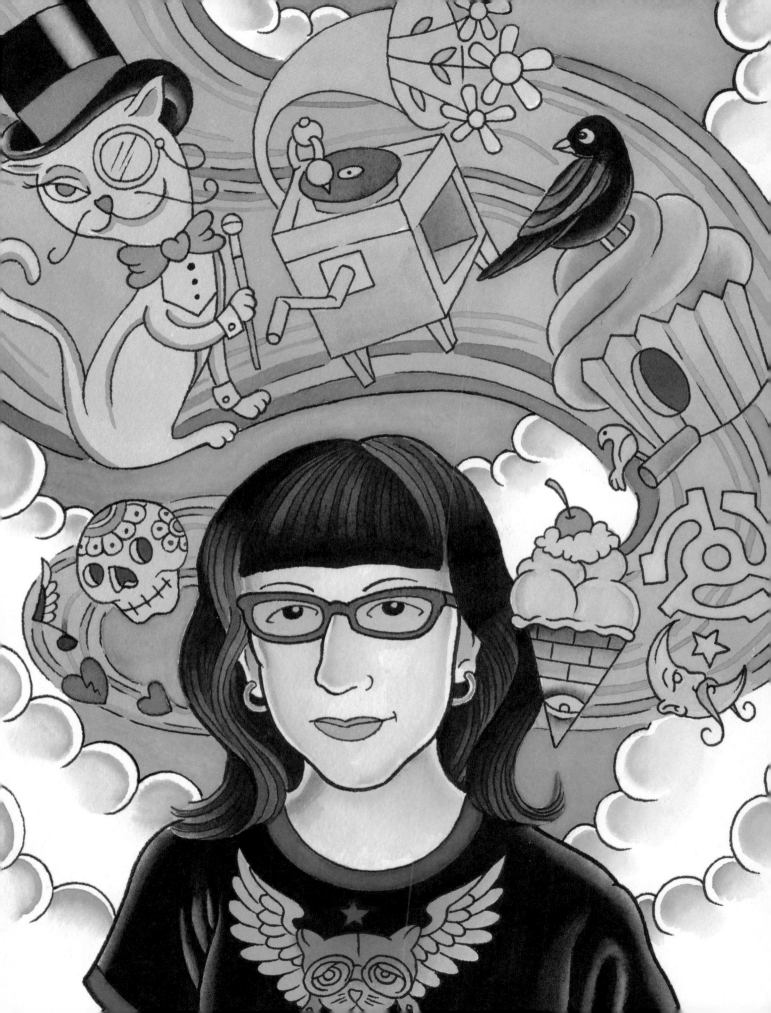

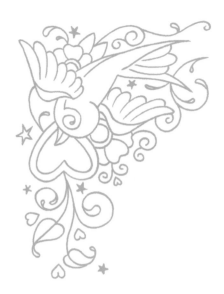

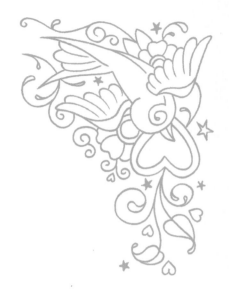

I did a little homework first,

to find the right tattoo shop for me.

A place that was clean and friendly,

just like a good shop should be.

Then I asked some people with nice tattoos,

"Hey, where'd you get yours done?"

"At the House Of Tattoo, ask for Katie," they said.

"You should go there to get one."

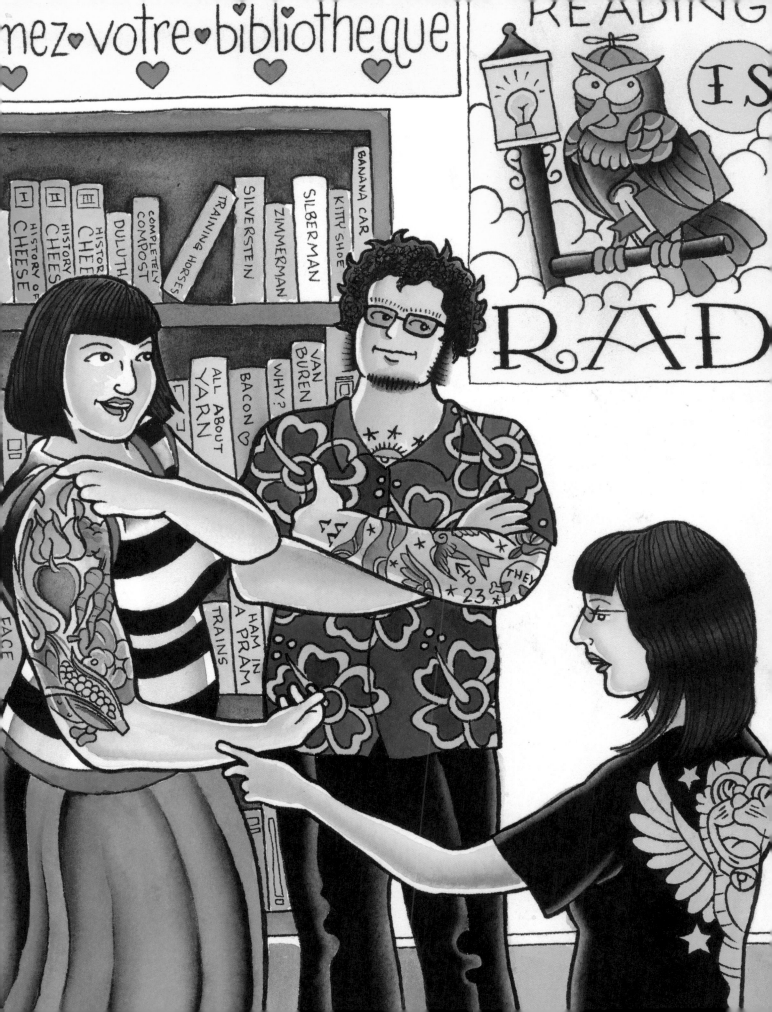

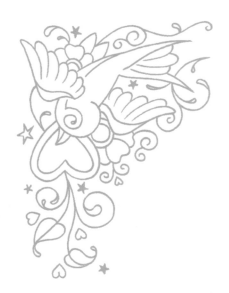
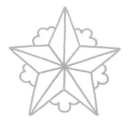
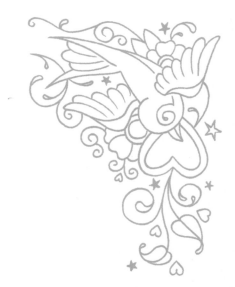

So I went all the way to Tacoma,

and asked for Katie by name.

A lady with grapes on her arms came out,

and said, "I am the same."

She showed me how clean her shop was,

and pictures of work she had done.

When I told her I was nervous, she said,

"It only hurts a little, we'll have fun."

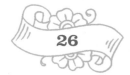
26

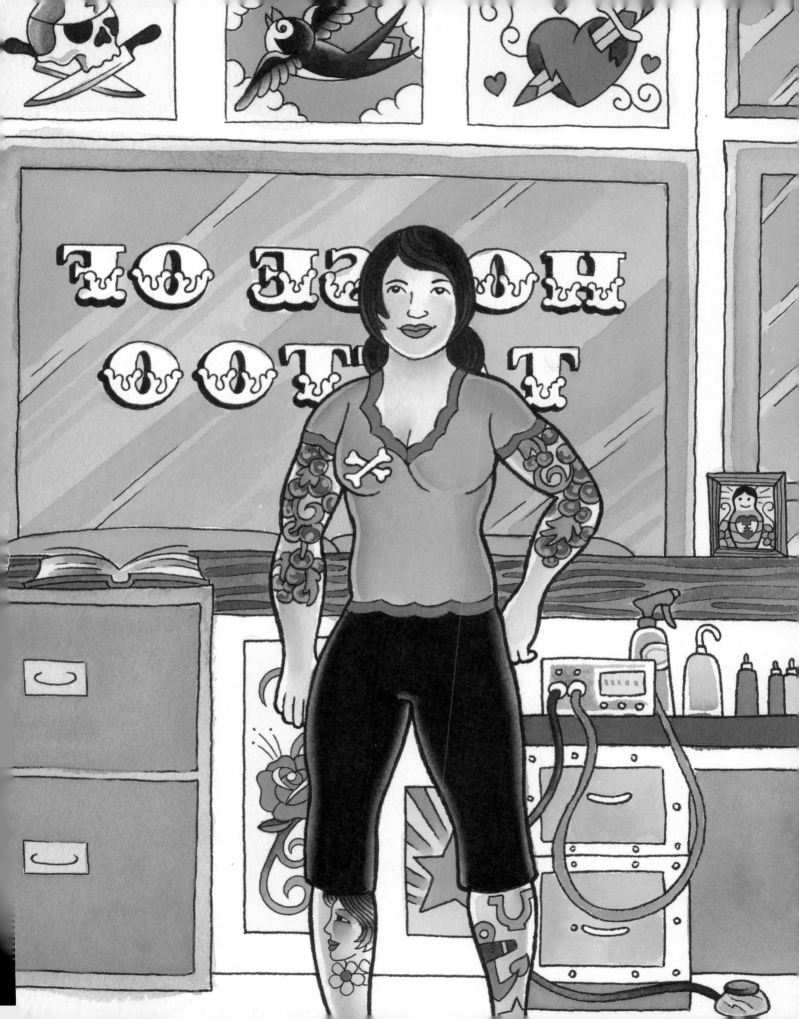

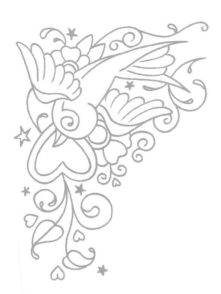

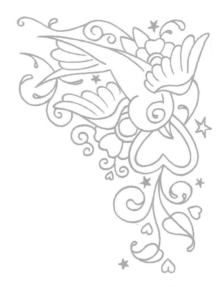

It felt like a cat scratch or a sunburn

when she put that tattoo on.

But it wasn't too bad, and I was so excited

to see it when it was done.

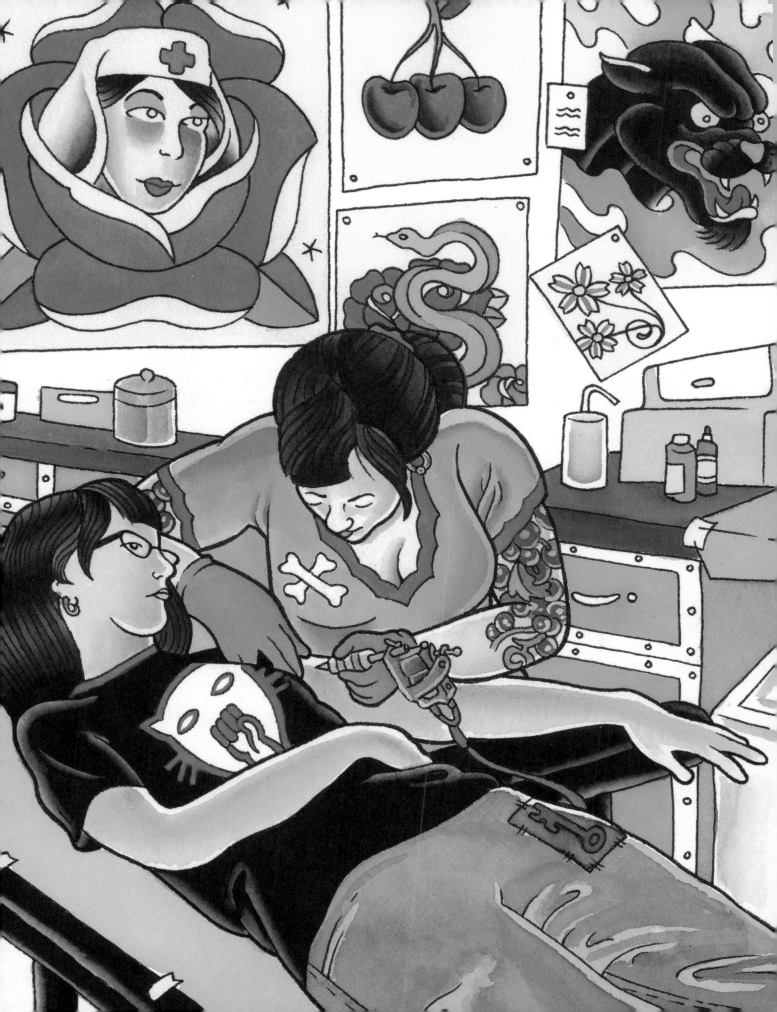

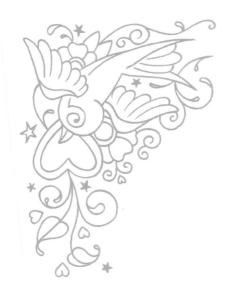

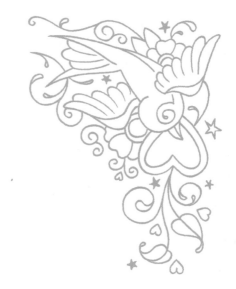

A little bird on a heart with some flowers,

and a banner that says Mother.

A tattoo just like my mom still wears,

and maybe in time, just maybe...

I'll think about getting another.

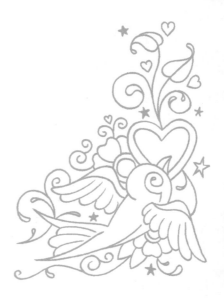

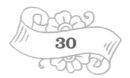

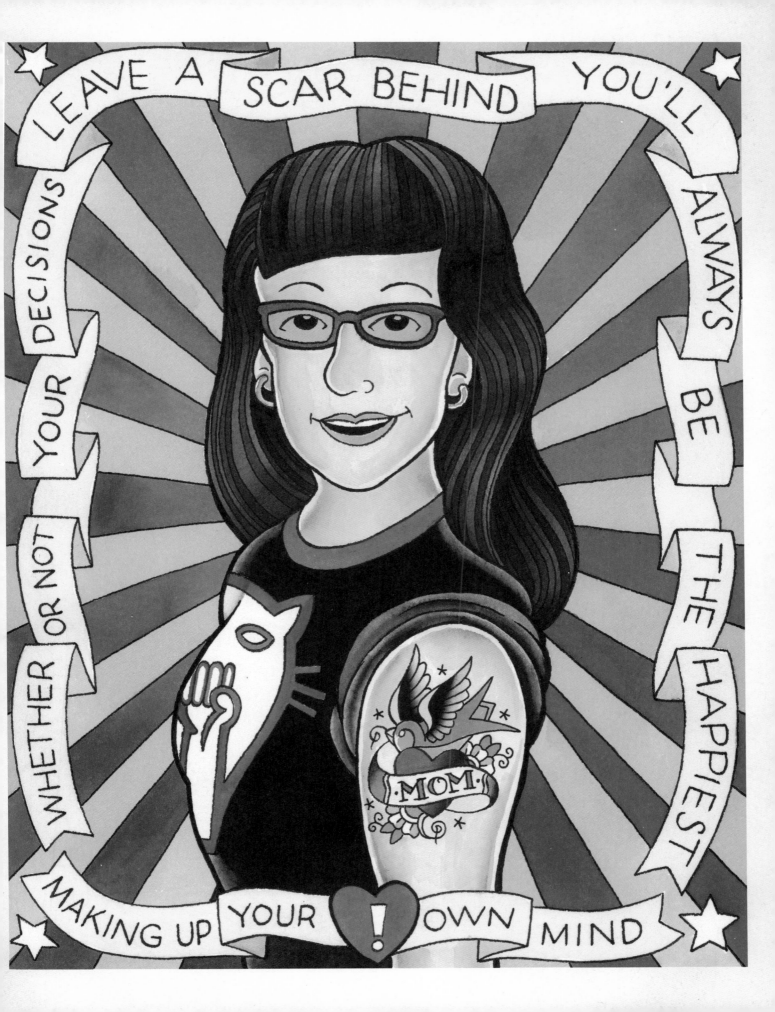

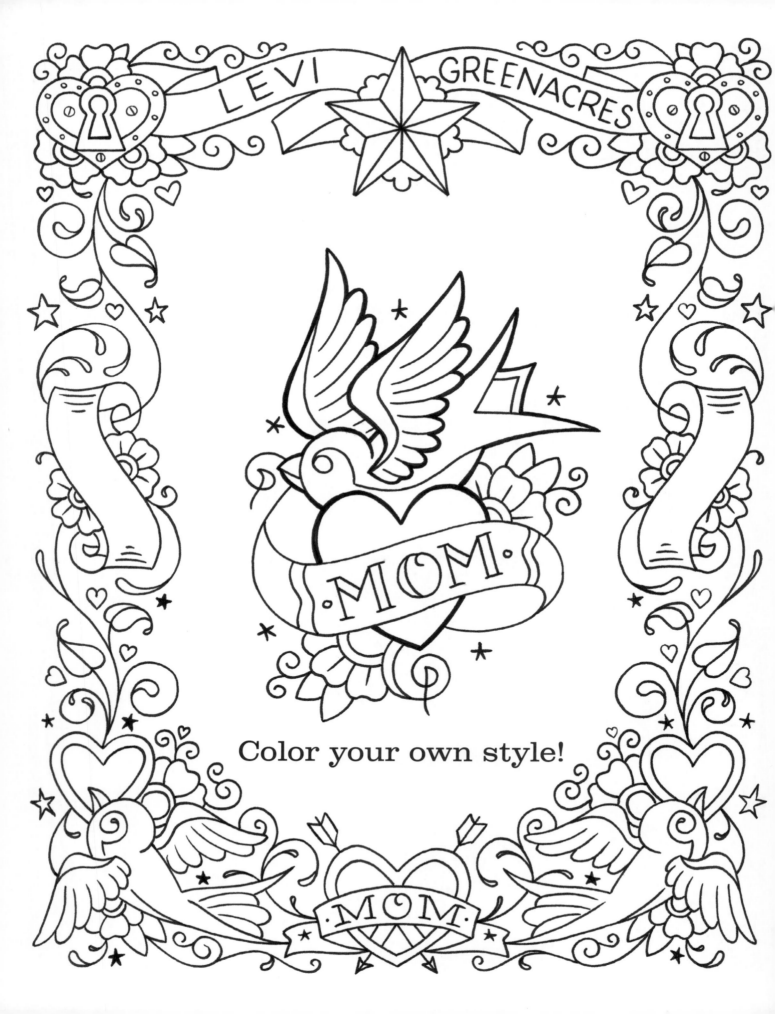

Color your own style!